AUGUST EXPLAINS

by PHIL RESSNER
pictures by CROSBY BONSALL

HARPER & ROW, PUBLISHERS, NEW YORK AND EVANSTON

For the baby

"I'm tired of eating honey all day and splashing in
the river," Ted said. "I'd like to be something else for
a change."

Ted was a young bear. He was resting in a tree and
talking to August, an old bear.

August was very intelligent and very good at magic
and tricks. "Well, what in the world would you rather
be?" he asked. Then he crossed his legs and leaned back
near the entrance of his cave.

"Well, I've been thinking it would be nice to be an elephant," Ted said, "but I just decided that I want to be a human being."

He jumped down out of the tree.

"That's what I want to be," he said.

"Hmm," August said. "Trouble is, I haven't turned anybody into a human being in years and years. I don't know if I remember how to do that."

Ted had not expected this. He sat down on an old tree trunk to think it over.

"As I remember it," August went on, "a human has to be able to *do* certain things."

"I can do all *sorts* of things," Ted said. "I can climb trees...and I can catch fish and..."

"Those are *bear* things, you ninny," August shouted.

"Well, I can do human things too," Ted shouted back.

"Maybe so," August said, "but little boys can do all *sorts* of difficult things."

"Would I be a little boy human?" Ted asked.

"Yes," August said. "Because you're just a young bear and…"

"But I'm big for my age," Ted interrupted.

"Don't interrupt," August said, interrupting. "Now, as I was saying, you're just a young cub. If I change you into a human, you'll be a young human—a boy."

"Oh," Ted said. "Well, what do boys do?"

August began to explain.

"First, they get up in the morning," he said. "Then they wash themselves all over."

"Hunh," Ted said to himself, "what's so hard about that?"

Then, aloud, he said: "I just jump into the old brook and…"

"Not the same thing at all," August said, waving his paw.

"Humans have this sort of a big pot thing. They fill it with water and they sit in it. Sometimes they have a thing that rains on them, and all the while they rub themselves all over with a slippery thing that foams up like a waterfall. Oh, it's terribly complicated."

"Gosh," Ted said. "*Then* what do they do?"

"Then they rub their teeth with a brush and some other foamy stuff. And so on."

"Boys do that every day?"

"That's right," August said. "And girls, too. And then, after they dress themselves…"

"What's 'dress'?" Ted asked.

"To dress means to put on clothes. Clothes are bags and things. Humans pull them over their heads and put their arms and legs into them. Then they close the bags with buttons and zippers."

"What are buttons and zippers?" Ted asked. He was very impressed.

"Well, I just happen to have a button here some-where," August said.

He got up and rummaged in a box on the floor of his cave.

"Ah, here it is," he said.

He drew out a big button and showed it to Ted.

"This is a very complicated thing," August said. "All humans have them all over their clothes. When they dress they have to push the buttons through little holes. Oh, it's awfully hard. I often wonder how they do it at all."

"And do they do that every day, too?" Ted asked.

"Sure thing," August said. "And then there are zippers. To be perfectly truthful, I don't quite understand everything about zippers." He scratched his nose. "Zippers are things you pull up and down. They make a very nice sound, like a sleepy bee. When you pull them up and down, they get stuck. Sometimes you pull them all the way up and you can't get them down, and sometimes you pull them all the way down and you can't get them up.

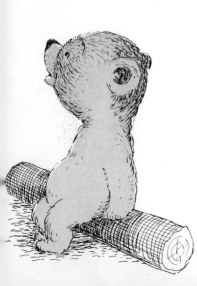

"But the shoelaces are the worst of all."

"What are shoelaces?" Ted asked.

"Shoelaces look like very long worms. Humans use them to keep their shoes from falling off."

"What are shoes?"

"Humans put shoes on their feet to keep them dry and warm. Shoes are like hollow feet."

Ted was listening with his mouth open. "Well," he said finally, "what do they do after they get dressed?"

"Oh, yes," August said. "After they get dressed they eat breakfast."

"Ah," Ted said, smiling again, "that's good."

"Yes, but that's complicated, too," August said. "For instance, humans use special things for picking up food and putting it in their mouths."

August thought for a moment. "Let me see. What *do* they call them? Shovels? No, no, that's not it at all." He scratched his head. "Ah, yes—spoons. Spoons and forks ...and knives. That's it: knives, forks, and spoons."

"Why don't they use their paws?" Ted asked.

August looked puzzled. "I guess they never thought of it," he said.

"One day some humans left a fork here in the woods. I think I stuck my nose a dozen times before I got that fork into my mouth. By that time I had dropped what I was eating."

"Oh, my," Ted said, getting up from his tree trunk. He came very close and looked at August's nose.

"Well, it wasn't so bad really," August said. "After all that trouble I wasn't hungry anyway."

"*Then* what do those boys and girls do?" Ted asked.

"After breakfast they go to school."

Ted started to say something, but August held up his paw.

"You want to know what school is," he said. "Um. Well, school is a place where children learn things. After they learn them the teacher asks questions like: 'If you have three bushels of potatoes and you eat one bushel, what do you have?'"

Ted thought for a moment. "I don't like potatoes," he said.

"That is *not* the answer," August said.

"After school, boys and girls go out and play. That's when they run up and down and hit a little ball with a stick. Sometimes they skitter around on little wheels or balance on big wheels. They do all sorts of difficult things like that."

"Gosh," Ted said.

"And then they do their homework," August said. "Homework is more of those questions like: 'Where is the best place to find honey?' 'What color is a brown bear?' 'Where is the Bering Sea?' And so on.

"After that, they go to bed. That's when they have
to do everything they do in the morning, only some of it
is backward: instead of dressing, they *undress*. Instead
of washing, they *unwash*. . . . Well, no, that's not quite
right; they have to wash *again*, and so on."

Ted looked a bit worried. He sat very quietly on the
tree trunk. He was thinking.

The only sound was the whooshing of the wind in
the trees.

The sun was going down.

It was getting dark.

August stood up and stretched. "I guess I'll start the
magic," he said. Then he dragged out a large iron pot.

"Before I turn you into a human being, I have to
make a big pot of magic potion. Now, let me see," he
said. "First thing we need is water."

He poured some water into the pot.

Ted sat on his log while August started a fire under the pot.

When the water started to boil, August threw a little of this and a little of that into the pot. After a few minutes he said: "Well, I guess that's just about ready. Are you ready, Ted?"

Ted took a deep breath. "I've been thinking it over,"
he said. "I've decided to stay a bear."

"Oh," August said as he stirred the pot. "I see."

Then Ted looked at his feet for a long time. He was embarrassed.

"I don't know how to do all that buttoning and zipping," he went on.

"I can't eat with a fork and go to school. Boys and girls must be very smart to be able to do all those hard things. I could never do them.

"I'm sorry I put you to the trouble of making the potion," he added.

"Well, no harm done," August said. "This potion is just as good as stew. Why don't you stay and have some?"

Ted was so glad to hear this that he laughed and did a little dance.

Then the two bears sat down together and started to
eat the stew.